Katrina Tears

by
Haley Moon

Wasteland Press
Shelbyville, KY USA
www.wastelandpress.net

Katrina Tears
by Haley Moon

ISBN13: 978-1-60047-094-3
ISBN 10: 1-60047-094-7
First Printing – April 2007

Printed in the U.S.A.

Katrina Tears is dedicated to my mother. Her strength after Hurricane Katrina was phenomenal. Alone she conquered circumstances that together a hundred people could never conquer. I owe her everything.

ACKNOWLEDGEMENTS

It is imperative that I recognize the hard work put forth by these people. They gave up their free time and traveled long distances for me and other victims of Hurricane Katrina. The numerous volunteer workers made life after Hurricane Katrina livable. Without their kindness, my home would have never been gutted or rebuilt. The same is true for so many other Katrina victims. Thank you all so much for your generosity. It is amazing the kindness you have shown and have continued to show years after Hurricane Katrina. None of her victims would have been fed, clothed, or sheltered without you. Thank you so much for your hard work!

My family was the vital component of my writing process. If it were not for their love and care I would not be alive and well. Their beauty has driven me to my best. My mother calmed me when I was stressed and my gramma encouraged me when I was ready to give up. It was their love that carried me through this difficult process.

All of the medical professionals that work each day helping children, teenagers, and adults, deserve a BIG THANK YOU! Their lives are spent caring for the world! I was given the chance to research and speak with such professionals who graciously shared their knowledge. It was amazing to be able to call upon such educated people as Dr. Marion Wainwright, Dr. Regina Mills, Dr. Kathryn Bush, Dr. Ginger Wishik, Dr. Richard Strebeck, Dr. Paul Matherne, and Dr. William Gasparrini. Thank you all very much for your time and generosity!

Of course I cannot go without thanking the people responsible for my literary knowledge. If it was not for my AP English teacher, Mrs. Linda Jordan, I would not have had the courage to write a book. She ignited my love for English and made me confident in my writing! My other AP English teacher, Mrs. Mickie Reed, drilled the numerous grammatical rules into my brain! If it was not for her daily grammatical corrections, my book would be illegible! Thank you Mrs. Jordan and Mrs. Reed!

The most tedious process of writing is the editing process. I must give a huge thank you to my many editors! Without my wonderful editors, this book would be filled with numerous grammatical errors. Hence, I would like to thank Mrs. Mickie Reed, Mrs. Susan Foy, Mrs. Linda Jordan, and Mrs. Stephanie Hernandez. Their guidance and encouragement was phenomenal! I also have to thank my student editors, Miss Jessica Kelley and Mister Jordan Lord. Their constructive criticism was greatly appreciated!

It is now the time to thank my friends. If it were not for one good friend, the pictures displayed within this book would be nonexistent. So thank you to Mrs. Melinda Spence for your kindness and patience. Our hours spent together choosing and editing pictures paid off. I could not have done it without you!

Thank you SO much to Mister Jonathan Coyle for his dedicated work on my cover. His photo shop skills are like no other I've seen! His eagerness to help me perfect my cover drawing was wonderful! Thank you Jonathan!

The encouragement I received from these great friends was tremendous. Their wonderful comments made me confident in my manuscript. They have been wonderful throughout my writing process, helping me before they even knew it. So thank you to Miss Morgan Ellis, Mrs. Cindy Ellis, and Ms. Claudia Burdette. Your love and kindness always motivates me to do better!

Everyday I am given support by my "little sister" and no matter what happens she always puts a smile on my face. Her beautiful heart always encourages me and helps me to see the beauty in life.

Thank you to ALL of my friends! You are ALL incredible people and I urge you to ALWAYS follow your heart. All of you are capable of anything. Without your love I would not be who I am today!

Most importantly, I owe a thank you to all of my brave peers, who without their courage, this book would have been impossible! Thank you to everyone who wrote an account about your life with depression or Hurricane Katrina. You are all so strong and your stories will now strengthen others! Thank you!

TABLE OF CONTENTS

FOREWORD

Whether you have chosen to read this book for the purpose of self-healing or for mere interest of the content, you have a great strength about you. You have put forth the effort and mustered the courage to acquire a deeper understanding of Hurricane Katrina and her lasting emotional effects, such as Posttraumatic Stress Disorder and Depression. I hope with all of my heart that the honest confessions of teenagers who have survived the nation's worst natural disaster and its difficult flood of emotions will assist you in your own emotional struggle, or complete your quest for knowledge on the subject.

CHAPTER ONE
Winds of Change: My Story

"Haley! Get up! Gramma had a stroke!
Stay in here with the dog. The ambulance is here."

Waking up to those words has always been my worst nightmare. Unfortunately, I was not dreaming. Holding our frightened poodle, Missy, I cried and sent text messages asking my friends to pray for my gramma. After what seemed like forever, my mother walked into my room and told me I could go into the den and see my gramma. Visions of my gramma lying helpless on the living room floor, as my pawpaw had six years before when he died from a massive heart attack, filled my head. So I shook my head no and remained on the bed crying with Missy.

The ambulance with my gramma inside made its way to the hospital. During the agonizing ride to the hospital, I prayed that the whole morning was a dream. Sadly, upon arriving at the hospital, I realized that my gramma's stroke was reality. My mother and I ran into the hospital and were directed to the waiting room where we impatiently waited to hear news about my gramma.

Finally we were able to go into the Emergency Room and stay with her. As I stood by her hospital bed, she began to cry. I have only seen my gramma cry once before and that was when my pawpaw died six years earlier. Seeing her tears absolutely broke my heart. More than anything I wanted to take this stroke from her, let her be happy again, and just see her smile, but all I could do was stand there. The Emergency Room doctor consoled my gramma, but I just stood there and looked on as my gramma cried. This reaction was so out of character for me. I'm always comforting my crying peers and bandag-

2

ing their torn skin, but for some reason I froze. It was as if I was paralyzed too, not from a stroke, of course, but emotionally. I was numb. I could not handle the enormity of the situation. My emotions were trying to catch up with the emotions of the moment at hand.

I could no longer bear to see my gramma in this condition, so my mom suggested I go home to let Missy outside. Missy is like my gramma's child, so she would be happy to know Missy was being cared for. Sadly for Missy, I had difficulty getting home. As soon as I got in the car, I began to cry. I broke down before I had driven two feet! So I went to the only place that gives me comfort, the stage, and thank God the Saenger Theatre is just down the street from the hospital. In the parking lot of my beloved theatre, I sat and hysterically cried for thirty minutes or so. When I finally calmed down, I decided to drive home. I pulled out of the parking lot and found a car driving towards me!!! I was so disoriented from crying that I had turned into the oncoming traffic! (DO NOT drive and cry at the same time!) Needless to say, this incident did not provide much comfort, so I returned to the theatre parking lot and continued to cry...

Undergoing intense physical therapy in a rehabilitation center, my gramma's speech soon returned to normal, and she gained some mobility on the paralyzed left side of her body. In late July, my gramma was able to return home. It was a complete role reversal. My gramma had always been my caretaker, and now it was my responsibility to care for her. It was so painful to see my gramma having difficulty with tasks that I take for granted, such as opening the refrigerator. My family began adjusting to our new way of life, and it seemed that we would be ok after all...

"Haley! Get up! You need to pack.
We have to leave. Katrina is a category 5!"

Sunday, August 28, 2005, my mother shook me awake. The morning was frantic. With the Weather Channel blaring in the background, I quickly packed. As opposed to the previous hurricanes, I packed very little because I usually brought tons of my belongings only to return home to an undamaged house. My mom moved plants around and boarded up the large windows. Then, she and I moved our heaviest table in front of double wooden doors. She moved my gramma's car to the street so no trees could damage it, and I parked my car in the garage.

After preparing our house for the category five hurricane, everyone piled in the car. With Bambam, our cat, Missy, my mom, my gramma, and me in tow, we began our four hour journey to my mawmaw's house in Natchez, Mississippi. As usual, the hurricane evacuation trip was spent listening to the weather station and hearing update after update about the hurricane. I assumed this hurricane would be like every other hurricane. I would miss a couple of days of school and return home to the life I left behind. Yet, this hurricane seemed different. There was an air of urgency everywhere. Gas was running out, houses were being boarded, interstates and highways were packed, and friends said their goodbyes.

Once we arrived at my mawmaw's house, my family was only interested in watching the weather channel, so I occupied my time by fighting with my fading cell phone signal. I would sit outside and text message as I watched the clouds quickly move through the sky like they do when a storm is coming. The night grew on, and we finally traded in the Weather Channel for sleep. Little did we know life can change overnight.

On August 29, 2005, just a day later, the worst natural disaster of the nation hit the Mississippi Gulf Coast. We woke up and watched the reports from the coast on television. The reporters were being blown around by incredible winds. People were being airlifted from the roofs of their flooding homes. Then, later in the day, the power went out. Thus, the only information we had was what I was told by friends who rode out the storm on the coast or who evacuated far enough away that the storm did not affect their power. More over, we could only communicate when the cell phone signal allowed us. The hurricane had destroyed most of the cell phone towers. As it was extremely difficult to acquire enough signal for a phone call, text messaging became the only connection to the outside world.

The text messages I would receive often read, "Haley, do not come back. It looks like a bomb went off. It's like World War II. Stay where you are." Friends of mine who were on the coast were living in their attics and wearing wet clothes from the storm. When volunteers made their way to the coast, my friends' only food source was the volunteers' meals or free MRE's (military dinners that only required water to make and contained two to three thousand calories in one meal).

With no power to run an air conditioner, it grew unbearably hot. This inescapable heat was detrimental to my grandmother's health, so my mom, my gramma, Missy, and I relocated to a historical hotel in Natchez that had had its power restored. (My mawmaw did not wish to leave her home, and Bambam does not do well in small areas like hotel rooms, so he stayed with my mawmaw.) This hotel was such a blessing. It was animal friendly and had an air of kindness that was like no other. A family agreed to trade rooms with us so that my gramma's handicap would be better accommodated. There were also many other hurricane evacuees residing there.

I continually heard news from my friends of their flooded homes or remaining slabs. It was so surreal to hear this from people whose houses I once stepped foot in. I found out that a building in which I spent my weekend before the hurricane was absolutely destroyed. The destruction was unfathomable. The previous hurricanes caused no damage to my home, but with the growing numbers of stories of destruction, I became worried.

Unfortunately, the Popp's Ferry bridge that travels over the Back Bay in Biloxi, Mississippi, not only had a boat resting on it, but was also missing a huge portion; and the road from the interstate that led to my house was covered with debris. Therefore, no one had access to my home until four days after the hurricane. A good friend of mine and his family were finally able to gain entrance into my neighborhood. His phone call was luckily one of the few that I received. He informed me that one of my front double wooden doors was lying in my neighbor's yard. Then, he told me my house had flooded and that the water line in my house was at five feet. I felt a sense of relief finally knowing the outcome of my house, but the reality of the damage did not set in until I saw it with my own eyes.

When the power was restored to all of Natchez, my family returned to my mawmaw's home. It was not until a week after the storm that my mom and I made the journey back to the coast. On the way home, we noticed the trees torn in half from tornadoes and missing shingles from roofs. But these sites did not prepare me for the devastation on the coast. Restaurants I had eaten in were no longer there. All that remained of them was a concrete slab. Debris was everywhere along the roads, and volunteer stations were set up in what seemed like every parking lot.

We pulled up to my house and immediately noticed the front yard that was decorated with miscellaneous objects such as five pound weights from the living room, a vacuum cleaner from the hall closet, and shoes from the closet in my room. I found an award for a football player that lives at least six houses down from me. It was unbelievable. Finally, we made our way into the house. I was not at all prepared for what I saw. The walls were covered with mold, and there was no light so a mildewy haze hung over our heads. (It was so creepy!)

To get to any of the bedrooms, I was forced to climb over a television, a chair, and tables; and with each step my foot sank into the sopping carpet. The bedrooms were disaster areas. In order to see the whole room, I stood on top of my dresser which had made its way under my bed. I climbed over my wet clothes and unsteady bed to reach my closet. Every article of clothing within it was covered in mold, including my mother's wedding dress.

I found my mother's room a mess as well. Her dresser had also found its way under her bed and her bed found its way into the wall. A reading cabinet was tipped over onto the leaning bed with glass shards and pictures littering the ground. Inside my mother's closet was the bag of family pictures and articles of every memory. I was determined to recover my beloved pictures, so ignoring my mother's disapproval; I climbed into her room and pulled the buried bag from her closet. All of the pictures were soaked and stuck together. As I peeled the pictures apart, I watched the ink disappear and held back tears. One picture that had not faded was a favorite of mine. It was a picture of me when I was Clara in *The Nutcracker*. I was ecstatic to have a saved this picture, but when I tried to remove it from its dilapidated cover, the ink smeared. I was crushed.

I finally made my way to my gramma's bedroom and saw her furniture in disarray. Immediately I began searching for her wedding ring. After her stroke, she had had to remove all of her rings because of swelling, and her wedding ring was in a crystal dish that sat on her now overturned dresser. She desperately wanted her ring and often asked about it, but it was no where to be found. I felt horrible.

The reality that my life had changed forever set in when I saw my mother cry. A picture frame holding a picture of her deceased father, my pawpaw, lay face down on his piano. As she lifted the frame from the buckling piano, water poured out from it, washing away the pigment of the picture. She was devastated, and there was no comfort I could provide.

Later, we were getting ready to eat our lunch of pea-nut butter sandwiches but we remembered that we had nothing to spread the peanut butter. We found a volun-teer station that was passing out free meals and joined the line of cars. As we approached the food tent, my mom began crying. I did not know why, and she would not say anything other than, "This is so nice." Eventually she told me that that was when it hit her that we had nothing, and she did not know what to do. She was re-sponsible for our family, and she did not know how to fix all of this. We finally reached the food tent and got our silverware. I felt guilty taking something from the volunteers. I thought to myself, "There are so many peo-ple who need this more than I do." I quickly remembered I was now one of those people who needed the donations more than anyone else. Never before had I imagined that searching for silverware, food, or free ice would be a way of living.

The afternoon soon turned to evening, and there was a six o' clock curfew we were unaware of. I had made arrangements with a friend in Long Beach to stay the night with her family, but at six o' clock we had just made our way to Gulfport. (The cities on the coast are arranged from East to West: Moss Point, Pascagoula, Gautier, Ocean Springs, D'Iberville, Biloxi, Gulfport, Long Beach, Pass Christian, Bay St. Louis, and Wave-land.) I began a desperate search for a friend in Gulfport who could house my mother and me. We actually considered sleeping in the car. It was at that instant that I knew we were really homeless. It was the most bizarre feeling in the world to be homeless. A week ago I had everything; now I was homeless and only had the few clothes I brought with me to Natchez...

My house was destroyed, my school was damaged, and my dance studio— which served as my second home— was damaged. My poor mother's classroom was, of course, one of the rooms that had received the most damage. My gramma's physical therapy clinic was destroyed, and she had to go without therapy for weeks. I was more upset when I found out that my dance studio had flooded than I was when I heard the news of my home. The studio gave me comfort and let me perfect my art, but I assumed it would be months before I danced there again. I began to abandon my dreams of dancing on Broadway, but I realized you can not forget a dream that is written on your heart.

I begged my mom to move to New York, but, needless to say, we did not. I had my friends with internet access find dance high schools in the South, for my mom would not let me go to a school north of Georgia (really limited my options). Deep down I knew I could not leave my family at this horrible time, but I wanted so desperately to dance.

It was as if our world had come crashing down on us.

School began just three weeks after the hurricane, leaving us no time to tend to our destroyed home. Rather, time was spent searching for a place to live. Luckily my grandparents on my dad's side had a neighbor who would be out of town for a while, so he let us rent his house. I was so glad we found a home so quickly and it was even handicap accessible! A couple of days before school started, we went back to Natchez and brought my gramma and the animals to the new house. My mother arranged in house physical therapy for my gramma, and she soon tried walking without a cane. It seemed as if the world did not hate us after all, but, oh, was I wrong!

I missed numerous days of school trying to gut (remove everything from inside) my house and I spent many weekends with kinds souls stripping my home (referred to as the "broken house") of its contents. The broken house resembled a sunken ship and produced nauseating odors. The more we cleaned, the more there was to be cleaned. My cousins and uncle removed the huge fallen oak tree from the top of our roof and patched up our roof where a tree limb had gone through. The jungle in the back yard transformed into a wild garden and then a dirty back yard. It did not seem like our house would ever be completed. (I wanted to tear it down and move, but my mother and gramma disagreed.)

Then one day my mother and I returned home to the rental house, and my gramma held open the storm door for us. I remember it as if it was yesterday. Missy had just run out of the house and down the steps. I caught her but had a book bag on my back and could barely move, so I sat down. My mom moved aside and I stood up. When I turned around my gramma was lying face down on the concrete slab. It was absolutely horrible. She had lost her balance and fallen straight down, inches away from slashing her head open on a stair railing. There she lay before me, completely immobile and helpless with small areas of blood. A neighbor was able to pick her up and set her on the couch as my mother called 911. I held back tears as I gathered materials to clean a scrape on her knee. I wished I had a medical degree so I could heal more than her scrape but I did not, so I continued cleaning her knee.

I hope no one has to experience the pain of watching a family member lie on the ground injured and completely helpless. The picture remains imprinted upon my brain and brings tears to my eyes each time I think of that day. She had finally begun walking on her own, and then she had such an awful fall. The doctors told us she had dislocated her right elbow, leaving her with only a functioning right leg (the stroke paralyzed the left side of her body).

Willingly, I missed more days of school to care for my gramma. I was determined not to allow Katrina or caring for my gramma to be an excuse for my grades to fall so I pushed myself to the breaking point. I allowed no time for myself to cope with the changes in my life and rarely thought about them. I quickly became obsessed with my weight and wanted NO body fat. Dance had begun two months after the storm, and every night after class I worked out at home for at least an hour and made a ritual of doing 600-1000 crunches everyday.

In October when I was shopping for a Homecoming dress there was a pooch in the dress I chose to purchase. The sales lady said to me, "If you lay off the McDonald's the pooch should go away." Well, I did not eat much fast food at the time so her comment did not help my weightless escapade. For the next week, I ran after school with the basketball team, attended cheerleading practice for two hours, danced until nine, and came home and worked out. I was also obsessed with calories and would not eat more than 1500 calories a day. On the night of Homecoming, the pooch was still there. Turns out the pooch on the dress was a result of the ribbing, not my body. (Fabrics are weird! Follow your own instructions for your body, not other people's!)

My tutu for the Holiday Ballet Gala (my dance studio's Christmas Ballet since Katrina ruined *The Nutcracker*) had to be taken in two additional inches from its previous alterations the week before. It was soon calculated that I missed more school than I attended, yet maintained the highest average in half of my classes. I thought everything was great! My grades were high, and my four foot eleven and a half frame was getting smaller.

Then, one night about six months after the hurricane, I had my first panic attack and cried for hours while hyperventilating (not a good mixture). It was triggered from stress because I had not yet read two chapters of a book for Chemistry, and I had a test on the chapters the next day. It was midnight and I wanted sleep, but I knew I needed to read the book. I began having trouble breathing and then began hysterically crying. The thought, "I just want to die," flew through my mind and scared me to death.

Following this night, I continued to have panic attacks at least twice a week. Seven months after the hurricane, the worst panic attack I have ever had came on the way home from dance. I was trying to decide if I should try out for cheerleading my senior year (it was the night before try outs), and I had cried so much my hands went numb. My mom almost had to take me to the hospital. Along with panic attacks, there were many times when I would become so upset I would just sit and cry with my mom until one or two in the morning asking her repetitively, "What is wrong with me?" only to receive the response, " I don't know sweetheart. I don't know."

Ironically, I am known as the smiley, bubbly girl, but my mother often pointed out to me that I no longer smiled. I was overcome with a feeling of utter worthlessness and self-hatred. I felt like I had nothing to offer the world. My self-confidence was non-existent and I would only accept negative thoughts about myself. I did not know myself anymore, and I felt as if I would never be happy again. Thoughts of death often went through my mind. I thought I could easily end the pain and unhappiness. I had actually convinced myself that no one liked me or wanted me around. I was unable to see that that was untrue.

Several times I asked my mother if I could go to therapy, and she made me an appointment. I knew this was a battle I could not win alone. It was one of the hardest things I have done to see a total stranger and tell her I wanted to die and cried all the time, but it was also one of the best things I have ever done. I was so afraid she would think I was "crazy." She reassured me, though, that I was not.

After several appointments with my physician, I mustered the courage to ask about depression. I was so ashamed to admit to her that I thought I had depression, but I am so glad I did. My mom had to tell her I was suicidal because I was too scared to say the words aloud. I felt like a puppy backed up in the corner trying to hide my face. Surprisingly, my physician had depression, too! She completely understood and was so supportive. It was wonderful! I asked her, "Does having depression make me crazy?" She said, "Absolutely not!" I felt so relieved! I finally felt like I might be happy again! I began medication and continued therapy.

A month or two later, about nine months after the hurricane, I had the worst night of my life. Before, I resisted the desire to die by remembering all of the teenagers I have helped through suicide and depression. If I committed suicide, I would make a hypocrite of myself. I knew I would be committing such a selfish act and devastate my family. However, as my depression grew more severe, I encountered the lowest point in my life, and everything that had previously kept me from killing myself did not matter anymore. The desire to die had overcome me. I cried hysterically and told my mom that I really wanted to kill myself and that I was terrified of myself. I could not trust myself anymore, because I desperately wanted to die. I did not know what was making me feel this way, and all I knew was that I was always sad, and I did not think I would ever know happiness again. That night I knew I was in need of serious help.

The next day I missed yet another day of school and saw an evaluator who asked me several questions. I did not know what he was or why I was there. He picked up on my confusion and told me he was deciding whether or not I should be admitted to a psychiatric hospital. I was floored. After the initial shock, I decided that that might be a good thing for me. He was rather confused with my case. I was telling him the plans I had concocted to kill myself, but was surprisingly perky. I was actually surprised at my perkiness as well. He consulted a psychiatrist and told him that I was suicidal but uncharacteristically perky for a depressed teenager. Nonetheless, the two decided that because I had gone as far as planning a way to kill myself, I should be admitted to the hospital immediately.

Everything was happening so fast. The reality that I, Haley Moon, was depressed, fixing to go to a hospital to be treated for suicide, was unreal. I wanted to go to the hospital because I wanted to improve my health and be happy again. I was exhausted from my battle with my emotions and was willing to do anything to make it easier. BUT it was the week before my recital. If I admitted myself into the hospital, I would miss a week of rehearsals and my recital. Dance is my love, my passion, my therapy. So after pleading with my mom, we decided I would stay home and perform in my recital; BUT afterwards, if I still needed to go to the hospital, I would admit myself.

Well, I never went to the hospital. The day of my evaluation was also the first recital rehearsal at the Saenger Theatre, the same theatre I escaped to when my gramma had her stroke. As soon as I sat down in a seat in the audience and watched the dancing on the stage before me, I felt perfectly happy. I told myself I would be ok. The stage is my comfort and it literally saved my life.

I continued therapy and medicinal treatment under the supervision of my doctor. I kept working out and eating hardly anything when, one week in the beginning of June, I gained about twenty pounds. Large, pink stretch marks covered my body, and my clothes no longer fit me. I had not changed my diet or workout schedule and could not account for this mysterious weight gain. All I could wear was sweats and t-shirts. My body had become such a focus of mine, when it changed uncontrollably, I was crushed. It was as if the more I worked out and the less I ate, the more weight I gained.

My physician thought my rapid weight gain could have been caused by my antidepressant, but I really liked this medication so we decided I should remain on the medication until my depression improved and worry about my weight later. However, my increased weight only depressed me more, so I ended up switching medications, and my mother made me an appointment with an endocrinologist, or hormone doctor. After tons of blood work and appointments with my endocrinologist, I was diagnosed with hypothyroidism, a thyroid disorder in which the thyroid does not produce enough thyroid hormone. Two major symptoms of hypothyroidism are depression and weight gain! I was glad to finally know what was going on with my body and began more medicinal treatments and took vitamins. This treatment is quite tedious because it requires constant blood work to check hormone levels for medicinal adjustments.

I suffer from what I like to call
Triple Whammy Depression.

Triple Whammy Depression is simply depression caused from three different things. It is clear that I suffered from Posttraumatic Stress Disorder with delayed onset (*discussed in Chapter Two*). I felt guilty for my gramma's stroke, fall, and sickness, and for my mom's immense responsibilities after the hurricane. I longed to fix everything for my family so that they could be happy again, but I was not physically able. Posttraumatic Stress Disorder causes an imbalance of chemicals in the brain that can easily result in depression, which I clearly developed.

Depression is a genetic trait in my family. Several of my family members battle with depression, and I have received their gene, making me more prone to developing the disease. Hypothyroidism, which many of my family members also suffer from, creates a chemical imbalance that often causes depression in people, such as myself.

Therefore, not only did I suffer from posttraumatic stress disorder, depression, and hypothyroidism, but my severe depression was caused by three severe disorders. I was being hit by something on every side of my body and feeling the emotional bruises. NO WONDER I WAS SO DEPRESSED!

The other symptoms of posttraumatic stress disorder, depression, and hypothyroidism that haunted me were lethargy, fatigue, and loss of motivation. Again I had a triple whammy suffering of these symptoms. It was the most horrible part of my whole experience. I was born with self-motivation. If there is something I want to do, I will work at it until I succeed. Because of these symptoms, the only thing I was motivated to do was sleep. I am used to constantly moving and doing something, but I no longer wished to do anything.

It has been a dream of mine to dance on Broadway since I went to New York City for the first time in eighth grade. Once my Triple Whammy Depression began, I seemed to lose interest in my passion. Dance has always served as my stress reliever and therapy, and it frightened me to think I did not love it anymore. So I comforted myself by remembering the loss of motivation for things I once loved was a major symptom of depression, posttraumatic stress disorder, AND hypothyroidism.

I believe that my fatigue and weight gain played a huge role in my loss of interest for dance as well. In the beginning of my senior year, I had not yet found the correct treatment for my hypothyroidism, and thus, was still gaining weight and extremely tired. I hated going to dance and standing before the mirror only to see my growing amount of body fat. It depressed me and started the whole vicious cycle over again! I was also suffering from lethargy, or an abnormal drowsiness. I would sleep all day and barely have the energy to stay awake for two hours. When school began, I could barely make it through the school day, let alone go to dance class. I remember my mom would have to run errands after school, and I would be so tired I could barely talk or lift my hand. I slept in the car all the way home. I did not have enough energy to work out and attempt to fight my weight gain or do the things I loved, such as dance. I was miserable.

Then, about a month ago, about eighteen months after the hurricane, I had another appointment with my endocrinologist. I begged her to increase the dosage of my thyroid medicine, and I have seen a tremendous change in my mood, energy level, and body. It was amazing! I have been chipper, calm (or calm for me because I am a naturally stressed out person), and I have been attending dance class every night, rehearsals during the day, school, weekend rehearsals, and writing!

This very moment I am not completely cured of depression, hypothyroidism, or posttraumatic stress disorder, but I am much better than I was a year ago. I have not had one panic attack since last year's cheerleading try outs. I am able to accept positive thoughts about myself, and, most of all, I do not wish to die. With continued therapy and medicinal treatments I know I will continue to get better. Even though my experience was very painful and life lasting, I am convinced I went through it for a reason. I am a much stronger person now and gained a great sense of self. Because of my weight gain, I realized my body would never stay the same or always look as I want it to, so I figured it would be a good opportunity to learn to love the person within it. I am still insecure at times and wish my body would be free of fat, but I know my self-worth is not based on my appearance. I am confident with who I am no matter how much body fat I have.

Now I know I can say I can handle myself emotionally. I know if I have a panic attack, I can deal with it. If I can not, I know what I need to do to fix it. I realize not everyone has as much family or friend support as I do, but it is so much easier to deal with any emotional disorder, especially depression, if you have someone to talk to. It is good to know that you are not alone in your battle. So if you do not have anyone to talk to, let my story and the other stories of adolescents' battles be your companion. We all know what you are going through and we support you.

"I've just come to a deeper realization of all that I've lost. My life of 17 years is basically over, and I hadn't even seen it coming. I wasn't prepared even minutely. I have never experienced a significant loss in my life until now— now that I've lost so much.

Yet I've retained so much more than so many people, but that doesn't make my grieving any easier. Thinking about and being reminded of those who lost as much as their lives just makes me feel worse, more depressed, and just guilty.

I had always assumed that certain things in my life would always be there. I know that isn't realistic, but a person just doesn't ever consider that major parts of their existence could be erased or wiped off the face of the planet by a massive force of nature in the form of a devastatingly major catastrophe. That is supposed to happen to other people.

My mind won't leave me alone."

~ Anthony, 18

CHAPTER TWO
Katrina Tears: Posttraumatic Stress Disorder

Posttraumatic Stress Disorder (PTSD) is an anxiety disorder in which an adolescent has been exposed to a traumatic event. A traumatic event is an experience that is emotionally painful, shocking, or distressing, where the adolescent's response involved intense fear, horror, or helplessness.

Several examples of common traumatic events among adolescents include:

- ✓ Natural disasters
- ✓ Date-rape
- ✓ Terrorism
- ✓ Child abuse
- ✓ Death

When an adolescent is traumatized by say, a hurricane, the memory is stored within the deep limbic system (discussed in Chapter Three) of the brain. A traumatic event creates excessive emotional stress, and sometimes physical stress, that if becomes too great can alter the chemicals in the brain, causing a chemical imbalance. This chemical imbalance could then lead to the development of depression (discussed in Chapter Four).

The adolescent may react to the traumatic event immediately, after several days, or even weeks and months later. After a traumatic event, adolescents may begin to lose trust in the adults surrounding them, have suicidal thoughts, or experience sleep disturbances. It is even quite common for adolescents to feel extreme guilt because they failed to prevent injury or loss of life (*Helping*).

"In the last days of August 2005, a hurricane hit the Mississippi Gulf Coast. Many people lost homes and jobs. I was lucky enough to have no damage. My house is near the bayou, so God must have been watching out for me. As I watched trees fall around me, I was thinking about everyone I knew and what was happening to them and their homes. After Katrina hit, I walked outside and I didn't think I was actually in Gulfport, Mississippi. No trees were left in my neighborhood. I know so many people who lost their homes were in shock. My sister, my mom, and I rode down the beach. We were so devastated. It brought tears to my eyes. As I wiped my face, I saw slabs throughout the beach. I thought, 'We don't deserve this.' I know we didn't.

On August 30, my birthday, I helped clean up the street and watched people throw out materials that had become wet. It was so upsetting. We had had so many hurricanes and only one other caused such a mess. I couldn't begin to understand the feeling I had watching people throw out such special possessions. I wanted to steadily cry everyday when I thought of how lucky I really was.

No one deserved to be hurt. And that day when Hurricane Katrina hit the Gulf Coast, so many were hurt. I don't know what it took for kids my age to handle their house becoming a slab. All of us in Gulfport, Biloxi, Long Beach, and the other cities need strength to rebuild our hometowns. To think what water did to us is unreal and still causes grief to many people.

My family didn't lose much, just memories. Before Katrina, I had two relatives who committed suicide, and during Katrina, their things were lost in my grandmother's destroyed home. I will never understand what people went through losing a home, but what I lived through, without any damage was one of the Gulf Coast's worst disasters to ever hit. That feeling I recognize. I know the feeling that says, 'God listened to my prayers.'"

~ Janie, 14

Treatment

Difficulty coping with a traumatic event can result in chronic conditions, such as depression (*discussed in Chapter Four*) and Posttraumatic Stress Disorder. Adolescents suffering from PTSD can heal without treatment, but some form of therapy is often required for healing to occur. PTSD is treated with special forms of psychotherapy, sometimes medications, and if needed, both. One of the most effective forms of psychotherapy used to treat PTSD is **Cognitive Behavioral Therapy (CBT)**. Through CBT, the adolescent is taught methods of overcoming depression or anxiety and how to cope with reminders of his or her traumatic events. Medications are often used to reduce symptoms, such as sleep disturbance and depression.

PTSD is diagnosed when the following symptoms have been present in an adolescent for more than one month:

- Poor concentration
- Sleep disturbances (nightmares)
- Difficulty falling asleep or staying asleep
- Irritability
- Little interest in usual activities
- Thoughts of having a short future
- Headaches
- Stomach aches
- Dizziness

Posttraumatic Stress Disorder is diagnosed as one of three forms. If an adolescent experiences the above symptoms for a period of less than three months, then the PTSD is diagnosed as **Acute PTSD**. If an adolescent experiences the above symptoms for three months or more, then the PTSD is diagnosed as **Chronic PTSD**. If an adolescent does not experience the above symptoms until at least six months after the traumatic event, then the PTSD is diagnosed as **PTSD with Delayed Onset**.

"I've just come to a deeper realization of all that I've lost. My life of 17 years is basically over, and I hadn't even seen it coming. I wasn't prepared even minutely. I have never experienced a significant loss in my life until now—now that I've lost so much.

Yet I've retained so much more than so many people, but that doesn't make my grieving any easier. Thinking about and being reminded of those who lost as much as their lives just makes me feel worse, more depressed, and just guilty.

I had always assumed that certain things in my life would always be there. I know that isn't realistic, but a person just doesn't ever consider that major parts of their existence could be erased or wiped off the face of the planet by a massive force of nature in the form of a devastatingly major catastrophe. That is supposed to happen to other people. My mind won't leave me alone.

This excerpt from my journal after Hurricane Katrina is representative of the many emotions I experienced after the storm. I, like countless others, was in an initial state of shock and disbelief that something so extreme had really happened, and that it had really happened to us.

However, the beginning shock was just that: the beginning. It had to eventually wear off, and the void that had been filled with my confusion was left empty again. With nothing else to occupy that vacant space in my psyche, depression invited itself into my life. Unable to focus, not wanting to eat, and feeling hopeless, I surrendered to my new companion and allowed the depression to completely overtake my weak and irrational existence.

Any other time in my life when something had gone wrong, I could always find someone else to pull me out of despair. Not only was this experience more traumatic than any other I'd ever had to confront, but it was one that I had to share with everyone I knew. I could not escape hearing about it; I could not find anyone to care primarily about my own frustrations because everyone was looking for an ear to listen to them; a hand to pull them out of their individual pits of despair. Even the adults in my life were frazzled. Every authority figure was distraught. Everyone was human. How was I supposed to cope with this when even the rational people had become irrational?

There are several solutions to coping; I employed many of them. I removed myself from the situation by physically relocating. I vented my frustrations to an uninvolved third party by journaling my feelings. I combated my mental demons with a defense force of an antidepressant. Yet, the greatest impact on healing my wounds has been from the passing of time. As the years go by, my wounds may eventually all heal, but I will always have a scar as a reminder of the bond I share with my old companion, Katrina, one that will never be broken."

~ Anthony, 18

"Before Katrina I had 4 best friends. We literally did everything together. However, after the storm, things changed. One of my friends lost everything and became depressed. Well... depressed may not be the word, but she changed. She started putting everyone around her down and started really caring about what everyone else thought. She suddenly was worried that because she didn't have all of her expensive clothes, we wouldn't like her anymore.

She was no longer the person we thought she was. She HAD to have the 'in' things to make her 'cool.' And she would only hang with the 'it' people. It changed our friendship and our lives. Now, when we see each other, we never even talk."

~ Audrina, 15

"Following the natural disaster, known as Hurricane Katrina, I was basically forced away from my home and was made to live in Jackson, Mississippi, to basically start a new life. My seventeenth birthday was spent away from all my family and friends. Instead it was spent grabbing my most valuable possessions from my home, and moving them up to my step-brother's house.

Not even three weeks later (having started at my new school for maybe three days) my step-father lost his year-long struggle with lung cancer (Mom said Katrina was the last bit of stress he could handle). It was then that I began to experience the lowest of the low.

It started off very mildly at first, just small bouts of sadness at random times (school, during meals, in the middle of the night trying to sleep). Insomnia set in, allowing me hours to think about things. I was kind of quiet at school, not really talking to many of the kids.

It became obvious to everyone but me after a few months that something was wrong.

It's kind of hard to explain what exactly I was feeling at the time. It wasn't always an extreme sadness, but usually the feeling that I was useless, that every little thing was useless. I couldn't do the things I used to love to do. After school, I'd simply drive my brother home, lock myself in my room until Mom came home, and then stay up all night on the computer (either writing or playing on the internet). It was like I didn't have the will to do anything.

I think even when I came down to visit the Coast my friends could tell something was different about me. It made me feel extremely lonely whenever I'd return to Jackson.

I'll admit, there were thoughts of suicide. It was almost a playful banter at first, but over time I actually considered the possibilities. In all honesty, it scared the crap out of me. I know I'd never actually go through with it, but the depth of which I considered it was scary.

I became this useless shell, cold to my classmates no matter how friendly they were to me. It was only by the grace of my mother that I returned to the Coast and slowly regained my feelings of happiness and normality.

I don't really know what would have happened had I remained in my depressive state. I probably would have turned to drug use or run off to the Coast on my own. (I considered it on many sleepless nights to simply grab my clothes and a few other things and just high-tail it down there. The only thing stopping me was the fact that I had only driven from the Coast once.) Either way it probably wouldn't have ended well."

~ Aaron, 18

"On August 29, 2005, my life changed forever. That day I lost my home and the homes of several of my best friends. I was in shock. It was so difficult to believe that the Friday night before we were at the first football game and then sitting on the beach talking about what would happen if we could not do that every week. I guess you could say we found out. It was difficult to believe that a little wind and water by the name of Hurricane Katrina could change everything we knew.

After the hurricane, it was a strange feeling, as if everything I knew did not matter anymore. I now knew what it meant to be homeless. I even understood what it was like to be churchless, like the people I helped in Saltillo every summer. I felt lost. For the first time, I was not in control and I did not have the answers. Everything was wrong.

I dug through the mud at my slab just like everyone else. I walked through the ghostlike hallways of my destroyed school and stood out-side of my gutted church. I walked through the debris at my friends' houses and found it eerily like the debris from mine. It was full of the nasti-est smelling muck and ruined everything you could have wanted to save.

It has taken a long time to recover from Katrina and we still have a long way to go. It has not been easy, but it has not been all nega-tive either. My friends and I are closer than ever. I have truly learned the importance of family. I have learned what it means to have nothing and as a result, have learned how much the kindness of others can do. Hurricane Katrina changed my life, definitely not for better but for good."

~Sarah, 17

"It all started on August 29, 2005. I woke up to my house shaking. It felt like it would crumble at any moment. The roof was shifting right above our heads. Everyone was scared, including me. I felt I had to hide my fear from my mother and sister. I looked out the window and saw nothing

but misery out there, with all of the debris getting thrown around. I could see my family's belongings being thrown around outside as well. Later, I looked out the window only to see my neighbor's house being destroyed by my belongings. I thought to myself, 'If we survive this, I will help anyone around me that needs help cleaning up and rebuilding.'

When the hurricane was finally over, I walked outside to pure destruction. At that moment, I fell into a small depression that would only grow over the following weeks after Katrina. I tried to keep it to myself and not let it show. I just went on helping others. I helped my neighbors clean up. It was extremely hot, and with no air conditioning and no power, we got at each other's throats many times. The whole time we were without power, so I could not get in touch with my family. It didn't help thinking bad thoughts. For the first night or two, it was really hard to sleep until I convinced myself to calm down and think that they were okay. It took about a week to get the power back on. I guess you can say we went through a week of hell and misery.

I knew everyone's life had changed forever when Katrina finally ended. The thing that was changed the most in my life, wasn't the surroundings, it was my religious life with God. After the hurricane, I started to slip away from God. I blamed Him for Katrina and everyone's misery. I stopped praying. I even tried to stop thinking about Him. It was really rough on me at that time. I felt like God didn't care about me and the Gulf Coast.

Afterwards, things started to get better. I went to adoration for a while and just talked to God. In adoration, a story came to mind where Satan saw one of God's faithful followers and he told Satan he only followed God because of the blessings He has given him. And that if God took them away, he would not follow Him. God heard of this and took away the man's blessings, but the man continued to follow Him. After I finished reading that, I realized that even though my 'things of importance' were destroyed, God will always be there and that He was the only important thing. With His help I was no longer depressed."

~Jerry, 16

"Some of the effects Hurricane Katrina had on me were depression and low self-esteem. It all started after the hurricane hit Mississippi and slowly went on by. I was with my grandfather, aunt, uncle, mother, my sister and her husband, and my dog. We were all stuck in a small hotel which lost its power and water after the hurricane hit. We had to ration our canned food and water in order to survive over the next couple of days.

My mother desperately wanted to go home and to her shrimp boat to make sure everything was ok. At the same time my sister and her husband wanted to leave and come back when everything calmed down. My grandfather, aunt, and uncle went to Alabama where my other relatives live.

My mother and I finally got to the Coast, but we were not able to get close to our house, for the roads that led south to the beach were blocked. We parked next to a drycleaners and tried our best to see the building we lived in. I felt terrible and started to cry because I didn't know what to do to make things all better for my mother. She felt she had lost everything that she had, because her building was her prized possession. My father bought it for her before he passed away. Trash and debris were everywhere on Jeff Davis Avenue in Long Beach, Mississippi. It was not only on that street, but everywhere.

We stayed at a friend of my mother's house for a week or so. They were lucky enough to have water and a generator for electricity. I felt so bad to show up on their doorstep, but we had nowhere else to go. I still thank the Lord that they were there to support us. I couldn't get any signal from my cell phone as I desperately tried to call my closest family, friends, and my boyfriend. I felt so hopeless and I knew I had taken everything for granted. I was finally able to get in touch with my sister and I told her that we needed gasoline, food, and a way to get away from the Coast. My mother was trying to get to New Orleans to reach her shrimp boat, but with my help and the help of my mother's friend, we changed her mind. At that time there were shootings, floods, and other sorts of things happening in New Orleans.

My sister finally came down to the coast and was able to pick up my mother and me. We rejoined my grandfather, aunt, and uncle at my relatives' house in Alabama. My relatives welcomed us with open arms and for a second I felt a little safe. I still tried to get in touch with the rest of my family, friends, and my boyfriend. Luckily, I was able to get in touch with some of them. We tried to hear any sort of news about the Coast's electricity. My mother and sister were able to get a job at David's Bridal and I was sort of forced to enroll in school in Madison, Alabama.

Like a little child on her first day of school, I felt so scared and shy. The school was about ten times bigger than my old school and there were way more people. I felt as if everyone was staring me down in the halls and classrooms. But everyone was actually quite friendly. They tried to help me out the best they could by offering me clothes, money, and help with school. I felt so welcomed, but for some reason I just could not open up.

My mother finally decided that once and for all she was going to go back to the Coast and clean up her building. She wanted me to stay in Alabama and finish school and I had no choice but to listen to her. I stayed in a room with my little cousin and my relatives treated me as if I was their new daughter. I tried to keep out of trouble and paid for all of the things that I needed. I got a job at Aéropostale to keep myself busy over the weekend and to support myself. For the holidays, I was able to go down to the coast to visit my family.

Surprisingly, I met my friend from the Coast during mass in Alabama. She was also going to school in Alabama. I was so surprised and excited that a familiar face was a city away from where I now lived. We spent time together and with other friends to keep our spirits high. We were even confirmed together!

Summer came around the corner and I was able to go home. I said my farewells to my relatives and I thanked them so many times for taking care of me. From time to time my sister and I take a trip up to Alabama to visit my relatives, especially my grandfather. Although I say that I was not really affected by the hurricane, inside there are painful memories that will stay with me forever."

~ Marie, 18

"I don't remember being that depressed after the storm was over but I do remember it getting really bad once I got back to school. I wasn't here for the actual hurricane, and I only remember crying just a few times. What really got to me was having to talk about it. I know it was better for everyone else, but honestly, it just made me depressed. I was thinking of everyone's problems, and it made me sad because there was nothing I could do to help any of these people.

Hearing about people having to swim out of their houses and tear holes in their roofs, just to stay alive, horrified me. At school we had to write reports and take interviews on the depressing subject. And, of course, when you saw an old friend, it was always, "So, how did your house do in the storm?" I didn't like talking about it in the first place, and now it was all people wanted to discuss!

Then one of my friends moved away and that was it. I was crushed. I couldn't stay happy. I would be upbeat for a few minutes and then be right back down again. My friend and I kept in touch and she was doing worse than I was, so I would talk to her about it, but it just made me sadder. It was almost like I needed to stop talking to everyone I knew to be happy again. At lunch, I would just sit there and stare out into the crowd of people and wonder how so many of them could just go on. I wondered how to be like them. So I started wondering if I had always thought like this. My friends noticed that I wasn't my usual perky self and they would ask me what was wrong, but I just mumbled that I was tired or something like that— not really wanting to admit that I was depressed.

It turned out that I, in fact, was depressed! My mom took me to Baton Rouge and I got some auditing*, and would go back and forth sometimes on the weekend and it really did help! Now I can talk about my friend moving away and other things that made me sad without feeling like I need to reach for a tissue!"

~ Lauren, 15

*Auditing means questioned and evaluated to determine and treat the said problem.

CHAPTER THREE
The Moment That Changed a Lifetime

Hurricane Katrina hit the Mississippi Gulf Coast on Monday August 29, 2005, destroying homes and bringing severe change to the lives of many. Katrina served as a predominant source of posttraumatic stress disorder and depression along the Gulf Coast. The emotional turmoil Hurricane Katrina caused was actually so great that the Federal Emergency Management Agency established a free counseling service to assist those in need. It is impossible to imagine the devastation that resulted from Katrina so I have included several photos of just some of the damage she caused.

According to the Harrison County Coroner, Gary Hargrove, the death tolls for Hurricane Katrina totaled 169 between Harrison, Hancock, and Jackson County. The death toll for Jackson County, which includes cities, such as, Moss Point, Pascagoula, Gautier, and Ocean Springs, is fourteen and there are two unidentified bodies. The death toll for Harrison County, which includes cities, such as, D'Iberville, Biloxi, Gulfport, and Long Beach, is ninety-seven and there are two unidentified bodies. The death toll for Hancock County, which includes cities, such as, Bay St. Louis, Waveland, and Pass Christian, is fifty-six.

Destruction Along the Gulf Coast in Mississippi

The historical Beauvoir home on the beach in Biloxi, Mississippi. Beauvoir is the home of the only Confederate President, Jefferson Davis.

The Spence home in Pass Christian, Mississippi.

Katrina actually moved this house in Gulfport, Mississippi,
from its foundation and placed it in the Bayou Bernard.

This home is accented with a pile of debris left by Katrina.

As you can see, the flooding waters have entered the garage of the house
on the right in Gulfport, Mississippi, and has almost reached the door
of the house on the left.

The right side of this house has not only completely collapsed,
but the first story has been gutted.

Saint Paul's Church in Pass Christian, Mississippi.

The inside of Saint Paul's Church in Pass Christian.
Notice that Jesus on the cross is one of the only things in tact.

A tourist attraction known as Marine Life Oceanarium that was located on the beach in Gulfport, Mississippi. The dolphins' tank was destroyed, and the dolphins miraculously survived in the Gulf of Mexico.

This home is in Pass Christian, Mississippi. Notice the miscellaneous objects in the yard, such as the large silver tube.

The common debris found inside a home after Katrina.

These apartments were on the beach in Pass Christian, Mississippi.
In front of the apartment sits someone's staircase.

One of the many slabs that were left after Katrina.

This home was completely gutted by the storm.

This home was also gutted by the storm.

Yet another gutted and debris covered home.

This is the Biloxi-Ocean Springs bridge that connects the cities of Biloxi
and Ocean Springs, Mississippi. The solid concrete bridge was effortlessly
broken into pieces by Katrina.

These pieces of destruction were once vehicles. Many car owners parked their cars in
deserted areas so they would remain safe from harm. Unfortunately, many car owners
returned home to find their vehicles in this state.

This is the Hardy Court Cinema in Gulfport, Mississippi, and yes, those are cars trapped beneath the caving roof.

My Neighborhood located in Biloxi, Mississippi

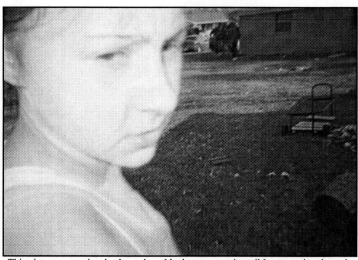

This picture mysteriously showed up. I had never seen it until I was sorting through pictures for this book. No one knows who took it or where it came from. The picture is of myself the first time I saw my house after the hurricane. My house was the victim of five feet of water. It is obvious I am absolutely devastated. This picture illustrates the feeling of someone turning my world upside down.

This is my kitchen, or what I like to call, "The Titanic." It smelled horrible!

This completely uprooted tree fell on top of my gramma's bedroom.
The fence is still on the ground that was pulled up with the tree.

This is my den, or what I like to call, "the furniture obstacle." To get to any other part of my house, you literally had to climb over the wet and moldy furniture.

This is my bedroom. My bed is sitting on top of my dresser, which when picked up fell apart. If you look closely you can see my lingerie cabinet (the tall skinny thing with drawers in the corner) falling apart.

The debris in a neighboring yard.

My neighbor's destroyed home and debris littered yard.

This is my best friend's home that is across the street from mine.
They also received about five feet of water and a yard decorated with debris.

This is the pile of my belongings that we had to throw out when we gutted my home.

My backyard, or what I like to call, "the jungle."

A neighbor's home that was gutted by Katrina.

This home was right on the Back Bay.
Katrina left nothing of it but the slab in the picture.

A home across the street from mine that was gutted and covered with debris.

CHAPTER FOUR
Teenage Tears: Depression at Work

Deadly
Energy-loss
Personal
Rigorous
Emotional
Sadness
Sickness
Imbalance
Obstacle
Not going to steal my life!

Depression is the most common mental health disorder in the United States among teenagers and adults. In fact, about **20%** of teenagers will experience depression before they reach adulthood and **70%** of teenagers with depression will have more than one episode of depression before adulthood. At any one time, about **5%** of teenagers are suffering from <u>major</u> depression.

As one of the most common emotional problems in the world today, **depression** is the result of a chemical imbalance of neurotransmitters in the brain causing a person to experience a somber mood that is persistent over a long period of time. **Neurotransmitters**, such as, serotonin, norepinephrine, and dopamine are the chemicals in the brain that give humans a sense of well-being (happiness). When any of these neurotransmitters are absent from the brain, a chemical imbalance occurs that results in depression.

Depression is more than feeling sad or down once in a while! This disease is a happiness thief, stealing happiness from adolescents' lives and replacing it with overwhelming feelings of worthlessness. Despite their **TRUE** value, depressed adolescents often feel utterly worthless and undeserving of love. They are incapable of seeing a bright future ahead and feel unable to improve anything.

"To me depression is not always this feeling of self righteous suicide. It's more of a self-lurking emptiness that is never filled."

~ Julie, 16

"Worthlessness is the most horrible feeling to be consumed with. I used to feel utterly worthless and undeserving of anything good. I tried to fight the horrid feeling and remember the wonderful aspects about me but the feeling of worthlessness won. As it took over my life I began thinking everyone hated me. In my mind I was worthless, stupid, and unlikable. Even worse, I thought I would never be happy again. I could not fathom ever coming out of this darkness. It seemed impossible to improve my life."

~ Michelle, 14

"It feels like you are imprisoned in your own body. For some reason, it is impossible to feel happiness anymore and you actually begin to feel unworthy of happiness."

~ Lindsey, 16

Along with mood, depression affects an adolescent's thoughts, thought process, and behavior. For example, adolescents with depression tend to have more severe negative and self-critical thoughts than the average insecure adolescent. Depression skews everything in an adolescent's outlook, making small problems seem large and impossible to deal with. These adolescents may cry over something as simple as breaking a nail or not being able to open their locker. Sometimes they may cry over nothing at all.

"I remember sitting in class when I would become so overcome with sadness, I would have to put my head down on my desk and have a secret cry. I did not know why I was sad but there was no happiness left inside of me, so I had to cry."

~ Kathy, 13

The central area of the brain involved in the depressed mood is known as "the deep limbic system," a phrase coined by Dr. Daniel G. Amen. Although the deep limbic system is about the size of a walnut, it includes the thalamic structures of the brain and the hypothalamus of the brain. It is these various structures within the deep limbic system that "set the emotional tone of the mind," record events as internally essential, control motivation, direct appetite and sleep cycles, and "promote bonding." Days filled with joy and cups that are half full are the days when an adolescent's deep limbic system is less active, providing the adolescent with a serene state of mind. Conversely, the days filled with the cloudiness of a somber mood and cups that are half empty, are the days when an adolescent's deep limbic system are overactive, providing the adolescent with a vulnerable state of mind. It is when the deep limbic system is inflamed that painful emotions compensate for the once happy emotions of a depressed adolescent. Thus, what triggers the inflammation must be diagnosed (Amen 37-38).

The numerous causes of depression vary among the adolescents who have encountered the dreadful disease. The normal stresses of life can easily cause adolescents to become sad, but it is alarming if these stresses cause an adolescent to remain sad for more than a period of two weeks or at the greatest, six months, time.

Something such as a breakup, doing poorly on a test, or not being chosen for a sport, can upset any adolescent, but these situations can also trigger depression in adolescents who have faced much rejection or those who are not accustomed to disappointment. Bullying and continual torment in combination with little or no self-confidence can trigger depression.

"When I was just a little kid, people were always teasing and picking on me for various [reasons]. But nothing compared to my 6th grade year, when my major depression started. I was finally in middle school and I was so excited to be there. But that is when peer pressure started, and all the clique chaos. I stopped caring about my grades and anything else important. All I worried about was fitting in with the 'popular group.' I was so depressed that nobody liked me, that I actually tried to kill myself."

~ Robert, 13

All adolescents have difficulty dealing with their changing body. The media and our peers force upon us body images that are unnatural or very difficult to obtain. Being constantly surrounded by big boobed female models who are stick thin, and huge biceped male models who have twelve packs, makes appreciating a changing body very difficult. Insecurities and low self-esteem often arise, that can eventually develop into depression.

"When I was 12 years old, I suffered from severe depression. It stemmed from being self conscious about my body. I did not want to attend gym class. Changing in front of a room full of girls who were all skinnier than me was horrifying. The weeks leading up to the new semester were too much for me to handle. I could no longer attend school. I would have anxiety attacks every night. They were so severe that I would hyperventilate and sob until my throat was raw. I could no longer handle the enormity of my depression and anxiety, so I decided the best way to fix it was to end my life. The night I had chosen to take my life had approached, and I wanted to give my mom one last hug. I walked down the hall and hugged her, and I realized, this would be the last time I'd ever get to hug my mom. I changed my mind that night, and within a couple of days, I told my doctor about wanting to end my life. She immediately admitted me to the hospital. I did out patient for 2 weeks, and I was ordered to go to school. That first day of school was torture. I screamed and cried,

begged and pleaded, anything I could do so I would not have to go to school. Nothing worked, and first period was gym. I was received with open arms by my classmates. All of them expressed their sympathy towards me and told me how much they missed me. I soon got over changing in front of everybody. We're all girls, and nobody stares. I went on medication and pretty soon all of my anxiety attacks subsided. I never want to go back to that time in my life. I am not ashamed of my past. It has helped me cope with other things that have come to me over the years. I am about to be a freshman in college and couldn't be happier. I still take anxiety medication; it has become part of my daily routine. I used to think that I was the only one of my friends who experienced anxiety and depression, but upon talking about my experience, I've learned that almost half of my friends have experienced the same thing and they too are on medication. I have become more comfortable with myself and am not nearly as self-conscious. I know that if I slip back into depression, I have friends who have had the same experiences and would do anything to help me out. I've learned to surround myself with people that I trust and feel comfortable with. Depression and anxiety have affected me, but it will not determine my life for me."

~ Sadie, 18

Other causes of depression include hormone disorders such as hypothyroidism, the most common thyroid disorder, and adrenal fatigue. Thyroid disorders occur within the butterfly shaped thyroid gland that is positioned towards the lower front of the neck. The thyroid produces and distributes small amounts of hormones through the bloodstream to EVERY cell within the body, so that ALL cells are able to function optimally. Adolescents cannot live without the thyroid hormone because it controls EVERY chemical reaction within EVERY organ of the body.

Hypothyroidism— note the pre-fix "hypo," meaning not enough— is the thyroid disorder in which the thyroid does not produce enough thyroid hormone. When deprived of these vital hormones, cells gradually cease their functions, resulting in a chemical imbalance (Lyness). This chemical imbalance could easily cause depression. Actually depression is one of the most common symptoms of thyroid disorders (Shames 16).

Other symptoms of hypothyroidism include:

- weight gain
- fluid retention
- fatigue
- difficulty learning
- irregular or heavy menstrual flow
- dry, itchy skin
- constipation

Adrenal Fatigue, also known as "Hypoadrenia" and "Hypoadrenalism," is a rarely diagnosed condition but has been one of the most recurrent conditions among people of all ages for the last fifty years. There are two adrenal glands in the human body. One pecan sized gland sits upon each kidney (there are two kidneys in the human body, one on the left and right side of the spine in between the rib cage and hip bone) controlling the way humans think and feel. The adrenal glands, or "glands of stress," enable the human body to handle stress from diseases, relationships, and problems at school. Adolescents can not live without their adrenal glands, because these glands release small amounts of steroid hormones throughout the body, providing adolescents with energy. When an adolescent participates in too much physical, emotional, or environmental stress, the adrenal glands are overworked, gradually lowering the amount of adrenal hormones released, in turn causing a chemical imbalance that could result in depression (Wilson 1-3).

Other symptoms of adrenal fatigue include:

- lethargy
- fatigue
- loss of motivation
- sensitivity to illness
- difficulty rising in the morning or not feeling fully awake until around 10 a.m.
- decreased tolerance
- increased difficulty dealing with stress
- loss of focus

Anyone who does not get enough relaxation to enjoy life, who is a perfectionist, or who has fought an emotional or physical illness is most likely already suffering from some degree of adrenal fatigue.

Depression can also be passed down in families as a genetic trait. It has been found that **20-50%** of teenagers with depression have a family member who suffers from depression or another mental disease. Thyroid disorders, such as hypothyroidism, can also be passed down in families as a genetic trait. However, there are adolescents with the genetic trait for depression or hypothyroidism who never develop the disease. Having the genetic trait for a disease does not guarantee that you will have disease, but makes you prone to developing it.

Depression in adolescents has been found most common in adolescents who do not have large families, are members of families who are impoverished, or whose parents are very critical. It has been found that adolescents who have a large family learn to accept disappointment better than those who have small families. For example, Vietnamese adolescents are least likely to have depression because their culture is very family oriented. Adolescents who belong to impoverished families are subject to suffering at home as well as teasing at school. This continual suffering, in combination with low self-esteem, often results in depression.

The upbringing of an adolescent also increases their chances of developing depression. Parents who raise their child to be "perfect" by making very high grades and simply being the best at everything bring depression upon their children. This constant criticism and pressure destroy an adolescent's self-confidence, making the adolescent more vulnerable to disappointment and rejection. Furthermore, adolescents who are criticized by either their parents or themselves, have an increased need to feel accepted and liked by others. If these adolescents are rejected by friends or lose a competition, the severe disappointment that follows could trigger depression.

"I remember I was sprawled out on the bathroom floor, hysterically crying my makeup off. As my mascara burned my eyes, I continued to text message my two best friends. The screen read, 'I cannot go to school here anymore. I'm

finding a new school. I won't be back next week. I can't.'

This was the first incident I can recall in which that horrible feeling of worthlessness overcame me. Prior to this cry session, I was attending a school party for our football team. When the students began dancing they formed this clump of people, which I found most difficult to enter. The clump would randomly leave the dance floor and migrate outside, then inside, then outside, then inside...I am not a follower. Thus, I did not partake in these 'follow the leader migrations.' However, throughout the night I grew more and more upset because I was excluded from the migrating clump. So, once the clump migrated inside again, I attempted to enter it. I was then pushed aside by a girl so that she and her friend could enter the dancing clump. I was enraged and devastated. How could someone so absentmindedly disregard a person like that?! I contained myself until I made my way home and lost it."

~ Haley, 17

Adolescent depression is much more common than people realize. Dr. Kathryn Bush, a psychologist on the Gulf Coast, said that forty percent of her practice is comprised of adolescents, and seventy five percent of those adolescents are receiving help with depression. Dr. Marion Wainwright, a doctor of Internal Medicine on the Gulf Coast said, "Being a teenager is tough! There are more pressures now than when I was a teenager…drugs, peer pressure, school, perfection, parental expectations, etc." Depressed adolescents often fear being labeled "crazy" so they do not tell anyone of their illness. When I told my close friends I had depression they were very supportive and did not think I was "crazy." I actually found out several of them suffered with depression as well! So for those suffering with depression, try your best to remember you are not "crazy." You are not responsible for the chemical imbalance in your brain and YOU ARE NOT less of a person for having depression!

I asked several doctors if having depression made an adolescent "crazy" and here are their responses:

- "Absolutely NOT!"
- "No!"
- "NO! Not at all. Depression is nothing to be ashamed of. It is a disease like any other. It just varies with how adolescents react to their environment, but no matter what, it does not make a person 'crazy'."

For years, the stigma of depression was that a depressed person was "crazy," which brought more shame to depressed individuals. However, depression became accepted about ten years ago when it was discovered that a chemical imbalance in the brain caused humans to become depressed. Before this discovery, society did not know nearly as much about the brain as they do now.

"I have no horrid natural disaster, traumatizing early childhood experience, or other such stereotypical factor to blame my depression on.

Mine is just simply that I'm depressed. After careful examination by 12 top notch psychiatrists over the course of 7 years, it was determined in the summer of '05 that the cause of my depression was officially 'unknown.'"

~ John, 16

FOR MORE INFORMATION ABOUT DEPRESSION VISIT www.medlineplus.gov!

CHAPTER FIVE
Suicide: Symptoms of Depression

The symptoms of depression vary from person to person, but regardless the severity, these symptoms are detrimental to an adolescent's confidence and happiness. At its worst, depression can generate such intense feeling of despair that a person contemplates suicide. Suicide is the most common symptom of <u>severe</u> depression and the 3rd leading cause of death among teenagers (Bates 22). In fact, suffering from depression can make an adolescent up to **12 times** more likely to attempt suicide.

Females attempt suicide **3 times** more often than males because females have larger deep limbic systems, making them more vulnerable to depression (*discussed in Chapter Three*); furthermore, they become even more vulnerable to the disease during times of significant hormonal changes, such as, puberty. However, **males'** suicide attempts are successful **3 more times** than **females'**, because of the violent means used my males (Amen 42-43).

"There isn't really a moment in my life where I'm able to pin point the exact instant when I became depressed. I believe that my whole life even until now I've been depressed. When I was younger over a period of five years I watched my father change from my 'daddy' into a psychopath, a monster whom still to this day I don't recognize. Being both verbally and physically abusive, he became the sole reason, I believe, for my descent into the darkest depths of depression.

When I was younger, years after the divorce, I didn't recognize within myself that there was something seriously wrong with me. However, I did know that for some reason every time when even just a thought would cross my mind of my father, I would begin to cry uncontrollably, and that's when the memories would resurface; memories of one of the most terrible nights in my life. The night when I witnessed my father threaten to kill my mother. He had a knife in his hand and he was pointing it at her and yelling (I don't remember what) and I remember that for some reason, I thought that I could save her, mind you I was four then so there wasn't much that I could do except for wrap my tiny arms around her legs and pray that it would be me instead of my 'mommy.' Luckily though, God kept him from killing her. I think God knew, like most people, that it would have been the end of me.

Though there's really only this one account of physical abuse, the verbal abuse didn't stop. After we moved out and my parents got divorced, I would see my father periodically. I hated going to see him. I was so afraid of him. When I was foolish enough to think that maybe I could be daddy's girl by spending time with him, he always proved me wrong by commenting on my physical appearance. A very touchy subject for a young girl, especially because I was no size two. It wasn't anything too horrible though, but just addressing it now and then led me to the point where I was afraid to eat in front of him, because I thought that if I didn't eat in front of him, he would forget how fat I was and then he would love me like I wanted him to. The comments never stopped, and when I was twelve I purged for the first time.

They say that people with eating disorders want control over something, anything, and there is nothing easier to control than what you eat, and they are right. I learned how to purge from a book my friend lent me, about a girl who became bulimic but stopped when she saw another girl that she knew almost die from anorexia; I had no example such as this. And I didn't want one. When I purged, I loved the feeling of being empty, because that is how I wanted to feel. I hated emotions, and I hated crying all the time to the point where I secretly attempted to kill myself three times. At this point in my life (I was around thirteen), I was so depressed, that I didn't care what happened to me, and I didn't think other people did either. I wasn't very liked by my classmates. I was made fun of constantly for being, what I thought, a feminist. I was angry and I wanted to die. I remember one day distinctly that I was outside walking to my first period class, and I just started weeping to the point where I just fell on the ground. One of the teachers was on his way to his classroom and he picked me up and asked me if I wanted to go see the spiritual director, and I said, 'yes.'

It was that 'yes' and the fact that I have kept on saying 'yes' that has led me to seek treatment, and finally begin to believe that life is livable without hurting myself and the ones that I love. Saying 'yes' to seeing the spiritual director that day, helped me say 'yes' to God, and to wanting help. Now, I'm not saying that I'm one hundred percent better. I'm still a little depressed, but I'm not taking it out on myself anymore. I still have those days where there's nothing I'd rather do than die, but they are few and far between. I believe in God enough to know that I do have a purpose, even though he hasn't quite revealed it to me yet. I know that He loves me and that others do as well. And it's this knowledge of all these things that I had to fight for, and, of course, the reason I am alive today."

~ Jacky, 18

The majority of adolescents interviewed after attempting suicide have said they were trying to escape a situation that seemed impossible to deal with. They said they were not wanting death but trying to escape bad thoughts or feelings and death seemed the only way to cope. Some adolescents who make suicide attempts may feel unloved and are trying to escape feelings of rejection, hurt, or shame, all of which are feelings brought on by depression. Adolescents who attempt suicide often feel they are a burden to others because depression made them feel unlikable and worthless (Nock).

"The day I longed to commit suicide was the worst day of my life. The only thoughts I had about myself were that I was worthless and a useless addition to the world. Before, as thoughts of suicide crept into my mind, I was able to remind myself it was the depression making me feel this way. I was able to see a glimmer of my talents and use to the world.

This night scared me to death because I realized I could no longer see that glimmer of my talents and use to the world, but only that I deserved to leave the earth and my family. I had convinced myself that I was only hurting them and they would be happier without me. These are the thoughts depression has the power to provoke in adolescents."

~ Haley, 17

Suicide attempts are not always planned in advance, but often occur impulsively. Dealing with situations such as a break up, a sudden moment of sadness, or a large fight with parents, while dealing with depression, can lead an adolescent to suicide.

Not all adolescents who attempt suicide actually mean to die. Some suicide attempts serve as a way for adolescents to convey the deep emotional pain they feel, but cannot describe, to those around them. Tragically, many adolescents who do not intend to kill themselves, end up critically ill or dead.

Signs that someone is contemplating or planning suicide:

⇒ Discussing death or suicide
⇒ Mentioning "going away"
⇒ Cutting themselves
⇒ Mentioning possessions they won't be "needing"
⇒ Giving away possessions
⇒ Isolating themselves from family and friends
⇒ Drinking alcohol
⇒ Taking drugs

If SOMEONE has told you they are contemplating suicide or planning to commit suicide, it is very important that you tell an adult. Even if the person has made you promise not to tell anyone, it is in their best interest that you tell an adult. If you fear you will lose their friendship by telling an adult that they are contemplating suicide, just remember that if you do not tell someone you may lose their friendship **permanently**. Suicide should not be taken lightly by anyone, for it is literally a matter of life and death.

If YOU are suicidal or have a FRIEND who is suicidal seek help IMMEDIATELY! You can even call a suicide crisis hotline, such as, 1-800-SUICIDE or 1-800-784-2433, or a local emergency number, such as, 911. These toll free hotlines are staffed 24 hours a day, 7 days a week with professionals who can help you figure out how to cope with difficult situations. All calls are confidential and you will receive professional help from someone who will never have to know your name! **THIS IS NOT SUFFICIENT TREATMENT FOR DEPRESSION OR SUICIDE!**

Depressed adolescents often fear their disease because they can not understand why their thoughts are so negative or why their actions are changing. For instance, an adolescent may begin to have problems in school due to skipping class, poor concentration, decreased or no motivation, or little mental and physical energy. Poor concentration combined with the negative thoughts caused by depression, often cause adolescents to falsely conclude they are stupid, hurting their deteriorating self-confidence even more. Unfortunately, because these problems only intensify their feeling of despair, some adolescents drop out of high school (Lyness). At this point in a teenager's depression, they are most likely experiencing several severe symptoms.

The physical symptoms of depression include:

- Upset stomach
- Loss of appetite
- Weight gain or weight loss
- Headaches
- Sleeping problems

"So, about a year ago I was dating this guy. I was head over heels for him, and it was one of those things when no one thought he was cute or couldn't see what I saw in him. Anyway, I grew up knowing this person, started to date him, and found out that he had some form of depression. He took medicine but if he missed it he got all sad on me, not wanting to talk. One day he told me it wasn't worth it, that the world was so screwed up, he wanted it to end...

A couple of months after that I found out that one of my friends was being raped by her grandfather since she was 12! She was 18 at the time...She was also on medication and seeing a therapist since she was suicidal because of depression.

Did you know that depression is one of the major killers among teens?

*I can't tell you what its like to be depressed but I can tell you that it's scary watching the people that you hold dearest to you go through it. It's one of those things that you can't do anything, **but be there**. You can't take the hurt away...even though you want to..."*

~Sarah, 15

Extreme lethargy is also a symptom of this disease, which often causes a withdrawal from people around the depressed adolescent. Relationships are often compromised when one adolescent is depressed, unless the other adolescent involved completely understands the feelings of depression. The isolation involved with depression is due to shame and fear. For most adolescents with depression are frightened of what could be wrong with them (Bates 18).

Coinciding with their low energy levels, depressed adolescents have little or no motivation to partake in the activities they once loved, which in turn causes more sadness and confusion. (It's a vicious cycle!) If you have experienced five or more of the above symptoms for at least two weeks, you should probably inform a trusted adult of how you feel so that you may be diagnosed and receive treatment!

If *any* of these symptoms sound familiar to you and you think you may have depression then take this depression self-examination! (There are many other self-examinations available online at www.medlineplus.gov as well!)

It has also been found that adolescents who have extreme feelings of ugliness or who have eating disorders could have undiagnosed depression.

DEPRESSION SELF-EXAMINATION

Circle Yes or No for your answer.

1) Have you lost interest in the things you once loved to do?

Yes   No

2) Do you have little or no motivation?

Yes   No

3) Have you experienced difficulty sleeping? Or have you slept more than usual (without increased activity)?

Yes   No

4) Has there been a change in your appetite resulting in weight loss or weight gain?

Yes   No

5) Do you cry 3 times or more a week?

Yes   No

6) Do you feel like it is impossible to be happy?

Yes   No

7) Have you thought about suicide?

Yes   No

8) Have you planned or attempted suicide?

Yes   No

9) Have you lost the desire to hang out with your friends or family?

Yes   No

10) Has it become more difficult for you to express or share your feelings?

Yes   No

11) Do you feel worthless or hate yourself?

Yes   No

12) Are you easily upset or irritated?

Yes   No

✓ If you answered YES to questions 5-7 it is very likely that you have depression or another emotional disorder and should consult a doctor or tell an adult

✓ If you answered YES to question 8 you have severe depression or another emotional disorder and should seek treatment immediately

✓ If you answered YES to 5 or more of the above questions it is likely that you have depression or another emotional disorder and should tell an adult

CHAPTER SIX
The Calm After The Storm:
Seeking Help For Depression

Depression is diagnosed by a doctor, nurse, psychologist, or social worker who assesses all of the symptoms of depression (*discussed in Chapter Five*), such as, emotion, appearance, and movement. The assessor will question and observe the patient, looking at the adolescent's posture, which is usually slouched in depressed adolescents. Sometimes the adolescent is unkept, with dirty hair and clothes, for he or she could care less about his or her appearance. Or the adolescent's movements may be slow because depression causes **psychomotor retardation**, or slowing of the psyche.

Symptoms of depression are present in an adolescent's voice as well. A depressed adolescent's voice is not perky and upbeat, but somber and monotone. Also, adolescents with depression are sometimes easily agitated and anxious. The diagnosis will include the type of depression the adolescent has and how it should be treated.

Doctors distinguish depression as either **Major depression**, the more severe but shorter lasting form of depression; or, **Dysthymia**, the less severe but longer lasting form of depression— about two percent of adolescents experience Dysthymia. Fifteen percent of adolescents with depression will eventually develop bipolar disorder (*Teenage*). **Bipolar disorder**, or **manic depressive illness**, is another type of depression that rotates periods of depression with periods of **mania**, meaning high mood and extreme bursts of unusual activity or energy (Lyness).

If you believe you are suffering from depression (a probable result of PTSD) or any other mental illness, it is vital that you seek treatment! **DO NOT ATTEMPT** to deal with it alone! There is not a cause or type of depression that cannot be treated. Sadly, less than **30%** of adolescents receive treatment for their depression, and untreated depression is the **#1** cause of suicide.

The most common treatment for depression includes talk therapy, medications, or a combination of both. **Talk therapy** with a mental health professional is a very effective treatment for depression because it helps adolescents understand the biological aspect of depression and how they can improve their livelihood. When medicine is prescribed for depression, the patient will be monitored until he she receives the correct dose or prescription. Because depression is caused by an imbalance of different chemicals, a patient may have to try several different medications, or amounts of medications, before finding the one that properly treats the correct chemicals, and the proper amount of those chemicals. The best treatment for depression depends on the severity, cause, or type of depression, and requires experimenting with certain medications and counseling.

There are many different types of counselors such as behaviorists and psychoanalysts who focus on various aspects of depression. **Behaviorists** work with depressed adolescents to alter their behavior, as opposed to deciphering and analyzing the cause of depression. **Psychoanalysts** help patients delve into their past in search of forgotten incidents that caused the patient's depression. This type of counseling is very difficult for adolescents, as they must analyze painful memories they attempted to forget. **Electro convulsive therapy** is a seven to ten day treatment that induces a seizure in the brain and corrects the neurotransmitters— side effects include Amnesia.

Psychiatric hospitals are available to children, teenagers, and adults who are severely depressed. These hospitals usually treat patients for a duration of two weeks at the minimum. Treatments provided in mental hospitals are very intense with strictly scheduled group counseling and independent counseling. In house doctors prescribe and monitor medications until the most effective medication is found. Once released from the mental hospital, a social worker may be assigned to the patient and will visit them regularly to make sure the patient continues to heal properly. The social worker can request a change in treatment if their patient is not improving.

Adolescents who are depressed should not wait for the sadness to vanish or attempt to treat their depression themselves, because it is impossible to treat this disease without professional help. Just as illnesses come about in the other organs of the body, depression is an illness of the brain. Luckily, most adolescents who receive help for their depression continue to live as happy adults, enjoying their life once again. It requires a great deal of love and support to make a full recovery from depression. It is for this reason that church leaders and family provide such a great support system for people with depression.

Dr. Marion Wainwright, doctor of Internal Medicine on the Gulf Coast said, "It is nothing to be ashamed of and is very difficult to deal with alone."

How an adolescent copes with his or her depression can result in life or death. There are several ways to deal with depression in a healthy, beneficial manner. For example, the most effective combination of treatments for continual improvement of depression is exercise, medication, and therapy. Exercise is a form of self-healing, as it increases the amount of neurotransmitters (*discussed in Chapter Four*), serotonin and norepinephrine, released in an adolescent's brain. Exercise also releases endorphins, which are neurotransmitters that provide a sense of wellbeing and pain relief, in the brain.

Adolescents who are unable to cope with the severe pain of depression may begin hurting themselves. Adolescents who cut themselves are attempting to deal with their inner pain in a physical way, escaping the mental process of dealing with their problems. The majority of depressed adolescents try to escape their feelings of despair by "drinking their problems away." Thirty percent of adolescents who are depressed attempt coping with their negative feelings through substance abuse, but this actually intensifies the depression (*Teenage*). Adolescents with alcohol or drug problems are more at risk for suicidal thinking and behavior, because alcohol and drugs have depressive effects on the brain. In fact, many suicide attempts occur when a person is under the influence of alcohol or drugs (Nock).

The best way to deal with your depression is by seeking treatment. Because I know how terribly frightening it is to admit your most awful inner feelings to your doctor (or anyone), I have included exactly what goes on in a doctor's appointment in which you are seeking help for depression or another mental illness. **First**, you must tell a trusted adult that you think you may have depression. **Second**, you or the adult should schedule an appointment with a physician or therapist. **Third**, you MUST attend the appointment!

KATRINA TEARS

The Appointment

At the appointment, the doctor will routinely ask you, "What is wrong?" Then you will reply, "I have been feeling down lately and I think I may have depression." You might be surprised to find that the doctor will not judge you in anyway, but begin talking to you about your feelings and family history.

Then, the doctor will evaluate your symptoms and ask if you have thought about committing suicide. It is of utmost importance that you answer *ALL* questions honestly. If you do not answer the questions honestly, you could receive the wrong diagnosis and treatment, OR no diagnosis at all! Finally, the doctor will give you a diagnosis and discuss your treatment options!☺

"After I was diagnosed with depression by my doctor, a sense of happiness that I had long forgotten suddenly overcame me. It was such a feeling of relief that my doctor knew the truth about my medical condition and I would soon begin treatment! For the first time I felt like my life would improve! I feel confident in saying that you will feel the same way!"

~ Elizabeth, 17

Finding the most effective treatment for your depression can be a long process, with the adjustments of medications and scheduling counseling, but it is worth it! Once you find the right medication and attend counseling, you are able to think clearly and love yourself once again!

"Through talk therapy I have been able to learn the scientific terms for my depressed emotions and damaged self-confidence. Learning about my disease helped me to realize that I was not 'crazy.' There were scientific terms invented to describe depression, so it must be a real disease that other real people have dealt with! Therapy has also helped me come to know myself. I evaluated who I am, my causes of depression, and how to deal with it!"

~ Allie, 16

If you are <u>ABSOLUTELY</u> not willing to talk to someone (a friend, parent, teacher, or any trusted adult) then writing poetry, prayers to God, music, or in a journal, is a good way for adolescents to cope with depression.

"I'm Not Alone"

*Counterfeit. I made a
Fake smile to cover
This one that I
Am ashamed of. I
Put on a happy face.
I clap my hands.
I am your
Sunshine. I set at night.*

KATRINA TEARS

Before I can sleep
I sit on
My bed and I
Cry for this,
And that, and
Everything and nothing.
I have no idea
Why the tears cascade
Down my cheeks and
Are dry by morning.
The next day,
You see me smile,
And you are fooled.
You would never have guessed.

~Elyse, 17

Helpful Hotlines

- Suicide Crisis Center ~ 1-800-SUICIDE (1-800-784-2433)
- Girls and Boys Town ~ 1-800-448-3000
- National Sexual Assault Hotline ~ 1-800-656-HOPE (1-800-656-4673)
- Childhelp Abuse Hotline ~ 1-800-4-A-CHILD (1-800-422-4453)
- National Domestic Violence ~ 1-800-799-SAFE (1-800-799-7233)
- National Runaway Switchboard ~ 1-800-621-4000

Closing Remarks

I am honestly a much stronger person now than I was two years ago. I feel empowered. I can now relate to and help other adolescents who are dealing with posttraumatic stress disorder and depression. Depression is a horrible experience I wish no one had to go through. BUT I have suffered through it and survived, so I know with all of my heart that YOU CAN SURVIVE TOO! Just hang on to that glimmer of hope long enough to seek treatment and deal with life as it comes to you. God has given us all one life. He believed YOU were special enough to create and He created YOU with a purpose. I want you to live and fulfill that purpose!

I strongly believe everything happens for a reason. So please believe me when I tell you this. You *can* survive depression and *you* can be happy again! If you need reassurance, just read through the numerous stories of others' battles with depression. It may now seem like your battle with depression is impossible to win, but in all actuality, you have the strength to win! So DO NOT give up your life to depression! I will be forever thankful to myself that I did not.

CHAPTER SEVEN
The Calm After the Storm:
One Day at a Time

Similar to recovering from a devastating storm, recovering from posttraumatic stress disorder or depression requires patience and living your life one day at a time.

Struggling with depression is a grueling and exhausting battle. There are days filled with little hope and days that are destroyed by sadness. A phrase that I have found helpful throughout my own battle is "one day at a time."

It is important to remember that school, activities, stress, hormones, etc. affect our emotions as well. All of these things can easily overwhelm us, therefore, bad days will always be expected. Do not forget that in addition to depression, we have everyday life to cope with!

In fact, just a few days ago I was so depressed and stressed that I broke down and cried. I was terrified I was falling back into my severely depressed mood (I had not had a break down in a long time), but shortly after my cry I felt like my perky self again. I realized that I was just seriously overwhelmed with school and needed a small breakdown to cope with my stress. This is why it is essential to take each day as it comes to you. It is perfectly fine if you occasionally breakdown and feel the need to cry; **BUT** it is when you constantly cry, become suicidal, and cannot imagine your life ever improving that you should seek help again or for the first time (Chapters Four, Five, and Six provide information about seeking help).

So whether you are rebuilding your home, your emotional life, or both, living life "one day at a time" will help you feel the calm after the storm.

REFERENCES

Amen, G. Daniel. *Change Your Brain Change Your Life.* New York, NY: Three Rivers Press, 1998.

Bates, Tony. *Understanding and Overcoming Depression.* Berkeley, CA: A division of Ten Speed Press, 2001.

Lyness, D' Arcy. *Depression.* 8 Sep. 2005. Online. Internet. 6 Nov.2006. Available http://kidshealth.org/PageManager.jsp?dn=KidsH ealth&lic=l&ps=207&cat_id=20123&art.

Nock, K. Matthew. *Suicide.* 7 Mar. 2006. Online. Internet. 6 Nov. 2006. Available http://kidshealth.org/PageManager.jsp?dn=KidsH ealth&lic=l&ps=207&cat_id=20448&art...

Shames, L. Richard and Karilee Halo Shames. *Thyroid Power.* New York, NY: Harper Collins Publishers Inc., 2001.

Teenage Depression Statistics. Online. Internet. 3 Dec. 2006. Available http://www.teendepression.org/articles5.html.

Wilson, L. James. *Adrenal Fatigue.* Petaluma, CA: Smart Publications, 2001.

BIBLIOGRAPHY

Bluestein, Jane and Eric Katz. *High School's Not For-ever*. Deerfield Beach, FL: HCI Teens, 2000.

Bush, Dr. Kathryn. Personal Interview. 29 Feb. 2007.

Gasparrini, Dr. William. Personal Interview. 5 Feb. 2007.

Guide to Depression- teenage depression. Online. Internet. 6 Nov. 2006. Available http://depression.prsto.com/?s=g&c=Depression-3&k=teenage%20depression&t=s&a=499...

Hargrove, Gary. Personal Interview. 15 Mar. 2007.

Helping Children After a Disaster. 12 July 2004. Online. Internet. 6 Nov. 2006. Available http://www.aacap.org/page.ww?section=Helping +Children+A...

Matherne, Dr. Paul. Personal Interview. 5 Feb. 2007.

Mills, Dr. Regina. Personal Interview. 12 Oct. 2006.

Posttraumatic Stress Disorder (PTSD). 18 Oct. 1999. Online. Internet. 6 Nov. 2006. Available http://www.aacap.org/page.ww?section=Facts+fo r+Families&na me=Posttraumatic+Stress...

Strebeck, Dr. Richard. Personal Interview. 5 Feb. 2007.

Understanding Child Traumatic Stress. Online. Internet. 6 Nov. 2006. Available http://www.nctsn.org/nccts/nav.do?pid=ctr_aud_ prnt_under

Wainwright, Dr. Marion. Personal Interview. 12 Oct. 2006.

Wishik, Dr. Ginger. Personal Interview. 28 Feb. 2007.

3 Nov. 2006. Online. Internet. 6 Nov. 2006. Available www.medlineplus.gov

Printed in the United States
86449LV00002BA/8/A